D0256806

For my mum and dad
(for putting up with me being frightened of jacket potatoes until I was ten)

A big thank you to Georgia Bickley for her lovely handlettering

First published in 2009 by Hodder Children's Books
Text and illustrations copyright © Alex T Smith 2009

Hodder Children's Books
338 Euston Road, London, NW1 3BH

Hodder Children's Books Australia
Level 17/207 Kent Street
Sydney, NSW 2000

The right of Alex T Smith to be identified as the author and the illustrator of this
Work has been asserted by him in accordance with the Copyright, Designs and Patents Act 1988.

All rights reserved

A catalogue record of this book is available from the British Library.

ISBN: 978 0 340 95983 1
10 9 8 7 6 5 4 3 2 1

Printed in China

Hodder Children's Books is a division of Hachette Children's Books
An Hachette Livre UK Company
www.hachettelivre.co.uk

Bella and Monty

A Hairy, Scary Night

Alex T. Smith

Bella Bones and Monty Mittens are best friends. They both like the colour orange. They both like slurping spaghetti. And they both have the same-sized feet.

But best friends
are **never**
exactly the same...

Bella isn't frightened of anything, but Monty is scared of absolutely everything!

bruises

lifts

ing

eons

spiders

cheese on toast

water

scrambled eggs

plugholes shadows mice woods

bananas swings night-time

bats

bugs

crocodiles

toilet flushes

owl

things that bounce

par

Especially the dark...

One sleepover, after a glass of milk and a bedtime story in their den, Bella switched the light off and they snuggled down in their sleeping bags.

'It's really dark!' whispered
Monty as his whiskers wobbled
and his tail quivered.

'Nothing is as scary as it seems,' Bella said, stepping out of her sleeping bag and leading Monty bravely into the night.

'Night has to be dark for a reason. The Sun gets tired from all the shining she has to do in the day. So at night the Moon takes over whilst the Sun has a snooze.'

Monty peered up into the
night sky and saw the Moon's
big face smiling down at him.

'Night doesn't seem so dark
and scary anymore,' he said
and helped Bella tuck the
Sun into bed.

A moment later though, Monty heard a loud groaning, moaning sound rumbling in the night air.

'Eek! I don't like ghosts and ghouls!' he cried with chattering teeth. 'They swoop into my room at night and scare me with their WOOOOOOOOOOOOOOOOOOOOOoing!'

'They're not wooooing at you!'
Bella explained.
'They are doing their homework
for Ghoul School.'

Monty took a deep breath
and followed Bella into class.

It wasn't scary at all! Bella
was soon helping a ghost
with a tricky sum and Monty
was helping a zombie glue
his ear back on.

Then, out of the corner of his eye, Monty saw something hairy and scary scuttling across the classroom floor.

'Aah! I don't like spiders!'
he cried. 'They come sneaking out at night and try to gobble me up!'

'Spiders are too small to
eat you,' said Bella.
'Anyway, everyone
knows they prefer
takeaway food.'

And Monty and Bella
helped a family of
spiders carry their meal
back to their web.

On the way home
Bella and Monty
walked through the
woods and Monty
didn't bat an eyelid!

He wasn't scared of
the hairy, scary
spiders. He wasn't
frightened of the
ghostly ghouls. And
he wasn't afraid of
the dark any more.

Back in their den, they nestled down into their sleeping bags.

'Bella?' whispered Monty ever so quietly. 'Are you sure there's nothing that frightens you?'

'AAAAAAaaaaaaahhhhh

Good night, sleep tight.